For Josie, who brought dogs back into my life,
and for Theo and Inky, unrepentant bed hogs
E. B.

To Marcel
A. W.

Text copyright © 2008 by Elizabeth Bluemle
Illustrations copyright © 2008 by Anne Wilsdorf

First edition 2008

Library of Congress Cataloging-in-Publication Data is available.

Library of Congress Catalog Card Number pending

ISBN 978-0-7636-2608-2

2 4 6 8 10 9 7 5 3

Printed in China

This book was typeset in Cushing Book.
The illustrations were done in watercolor.

Candlewick Press
2067 Massachusetts Avenue
Cambridge, Massachusetts 02140

visit us at www.candlewick.com

Dogs on the Bed

Elizabeth Bluemle

illustrated by

Anne Wilsdorf

CANDLEWICK PRESS
CAMBRIDGE, MASSACHUSETTS

There are dogs on the bed
Like logs on the bed
Bed hogs on the bed—
These dogs, these dogs!

Sideways on the bed
Dog maze on the bed

Paws grazing our heads—
These dogs, these dogs.

Here's another tailywagger made of fur
Snoozing in the center of the comforter

Tiny little doggie barely weighs ten pounds—
Suddenly as heavy as a basset hound!

These dogs on the bed
Bring clogs on the bed
Chew slippers instead
Of bones—these dogs.

Piled up in a heap
They're stacked five deep
We can't get to sleep
For dogs, these dogs.

Join us in a doggie-dancing rodeo!
Watch them hop to-and-fro-deo

Vying for a spot on Daddy's pill-e-ow—
Daddy's gonna give 'em all the old heave-ho!

Now banished, they lie
They pout and they sigh
And give us the eye—
These dogs, these dogs.

They go on the prowl
They bark and they growl
Night sounds make them howl—
These dogs, these dogs.

Now they're scratching at the door.
Mom lets them win.
Out they go. Doggies grin.

Thirty seconds later they want right back in—
Mom's become the doorman of the In-Out Inn!

Now back on the bed
They shed on the spread
Their snores wake the dead—
These doggone dogs.

They stick out their paws

And drool out their jaws

There oughtta be laws
For dogs, these dogs!

When we get too sleepy,
here's their sneaky plan:
Push us off if they can.

Nudge a little, shove a little, man oh man—
Suddenly we're cuddling the ottoman.

We're folks on the floor
With legroom galore
But chilled to the core
Are folks, we folks.

The dogs gather 'round
Our camp on the ground
Dog "blankets" abound—
Our dogs, these dogs.

So dogs on the bed
Aren't always so bad
I guess we've been had
By dogs, these dogs!

As portable heat
They just can't be beat
It's worth losing sheet
to dogs, these dogs—

It's worth sharing sleep with dogs.